Miraj

A fable about Addiction by

Dr. A. Sadah

*To my patients who I have seen
struggle through addiction.*

Tim lived in the forest in a small and beautiful cottage. He was spontaneous, driven by curiosity and a love for adventure. He enjoyed walking in the forest to discover new places and things. He liked finding new trees, flowers, birds, and animals. He was a lumberjack by trade.

Like everybody else, Tim had daily chores to do. He had to make his bed, clean his cottage, water the flowers, feed the chickens and his goldfish Wysmin, prepare his meal, collect and cut wood to sell, fix things when they occasionally break, and other mundane tasks. But some days he disliked having to do all that. In fact, he sometimes felt bored and stressed out by these daily chores. He occasionally made excuses to himself to avoid or postpone doing them but most days he managed to complete them before the day was over.

His family and friends lived in a town outside the forest. He enjoyed visiting them at least monthly especially if he felt lonely. But he got anxious and uncomfortable in a big group of people and often preferred feeling lonely over stepping outside his comfort zone. Family and friends wanted to connect with him more, but they did not want him to feel uncomfortable, so they understood whenever he decided to leave.

Wysmin, the goldfish was his closest friend. He admired how content and calm he seemed and often shared his thoughts and feelings with him at the end of the day.

Life was boring and uncomfortable sometimes, but mostly it was okay even though he yearned for more excitement and new experiences. He rarely felt joy from the mundane experiences of everyday life. It seemed as if there was something missing in his world, something that would spark motivation and excitement and make him feel complete.

Boredom, stress, loneliness, anxiety, and depression are some of the things that create voids in our life. Voids attract habits to fill them. Habits can be good or bad. Novelty-seeking, impulsivity, and risk-taking are personality traits that make one susceptible to getting hooked on things.

One day, he was feeling bored and stressed out with his chores so he decided to go hiking in the forest. Something amazing happened! He came across a small, cute, but odd-looking creature playing between the trees. Tim instantly felt curious. The creature looked like a mixture between a rabbit and a baby dragon. Covered with soft purple fur, he found it very tempting to touch. He got closer and noticed an innocent-looking creature with a welcoming face and mutual curiosity! Tim could swear that the creature was smiling at him! It seemed to read Tim's feelings and respond to Tim's facial expressions and body language. Tim tried to communicate with gestures and words. Surprisingly, the creature seemed to understand him and respond by jumping and smiling. WOW! This is AMAZING! he thought to himself. He was no longer thinking about his work that day and the chores he had to do. For a short time, he was flooded with joy and felt stress-free. They played together for the next few hours until Tim went back home for dinner.

That night, he fell asleep while thinking about all the possibilities of his discovery. Will this new friend understand all his thoughts and feelings? Will it keep him company and keep him from feeling bored and lonely again? How can this friendship help him be more confident and successful? He had a strange dream that night. His new friend was talking and Tim could understand him. The creature said his name was Miraj, and that he would make Tim happy and resolve all of his problems and all the problems he would ever face. In the dream, Tim became rich, popular, strong, confident, calm and full of energy and excitement. He found happiness everywhere around him! What a strange and beautiful dream!

The next morning, he woke up in a good mood and went outside to collect wood. Every now and then, he thought about his new friend and wondered what he might be doing. Tim found himself wandering in the same area he met him the day before hoping to accidentally encounter him again. It was not long before they bumped into each other. That day, Tim decided to name the creature Miraj like in his dream. Miraj seemed happy to see Tim. This time they interacted more. They played together, chased each other around, and climbed trees. They spent hours together and the time flew by. Something felt magical and perfect when they were together!

Because it was late, he had to stop and collect more wood before the day ended. After all, he still had work to do! He hesitantly said goodbye to Miraj and spent the rest of the day

catching up on work and thinking about how much fun he had earlier.

Over the next several weeks, Tim and Miraj met frequently and spent hours together every time. Increasingly, Tim felt that Miraj understood him well and tuned in to his feelings. Miraj seemed to easily read Tim's mind and make him laugh. Miraj came up with new games and showed Tim new places to discover. They now spoke the same language and enjoyed eating a meal together every day. Miraj's company took away the stress and boredom that Tim had. Gradually, they spent more time together on a regular basis. Tim had to work harder and sometimes into the evening to make up for the time he spent with Miraj.

The more rewarding the experience the more likely it is going to be wanted again and the more likely it will happen. The more it happens, the less effort it will take in future occurrences until it becomes automatic and happens without much thought or effort.

The habit is born

For some time, Tim was convinced that Miraj was making him happier, more productive, and more energetic. Tim assumed that he needed Miraj to continue feeling that way. He tried to do his chores faster in order to make more time to meet and play together. As the weeks and months went by, spending time together became an essential part of Tim's life. It was expected and needed without much questioning or thinking. He found it hard to wake up and work on the days he didn't see Miraj. On those days, the same daily chores felt even more tiring and more boring than usual. It seemed that he was doing the bare minimum of what was required to maintain his life while trying to maximize the time with Miraj. His motivation to do anything else was decreasing. These meetings became an integral part of Tim's daily routine. In fact, they needed to be longer to reach the same level of excitement and pleasure as in the beginning. Other activities had to be rescheduled around these meetings. At times he forgot or skipped the daily tasks such as watering the flowers in the garden and cleaning his place. By this time, his visits to his family and friends became shorter and far in between. His family noticed that he was distracted and impatient whenever he visited them. He even became irritable with them when they asked for his help which was unusual for him. He felt that Miraj's company was more important than any other relationship in his life. He became preoccupied with it so much that he stopped talking to Wysmin and forgot to feed him until one day he died!

Without regular care and feeding, the chickens also became thin and laid fewer eggs. He had no idea that his friends and family missed him and were concerned about him. He did notice, however, that Miraj was quickly growing in size and having bigger muscles. He was bringing him food every day. They ate one or two meals together but Miraj seemed to get bigger every day and eat more food. Gradually, there was less food left for Tim.

*Addiction integrates into one's life and becomes
an automatic habit.*

*Addictive habits increasingly consume important resources like time,
energy, and money. Addiction slowly grows at the expense of other
aspects of life such as healthy relationships, work, and self-care.
Addiction may initially seem to help productivity,
but it always ends up hurting it.*

Tim's family and friends tried fruitlessly many times to connect with him. They missed him and wondered about him but he was unaware of their concerns. His awareness of time and other people in his life gradually changed. His daily routine revolved around his relationship with Miraj. Everything else was less important. The first thing he thought about when he woke up every morning was how to meet with Miraj and how to come up with food and time to feed him. Some days he felt good when they met, and some days he did not. But in both cases, he felt somehow compelled to meet him. He did not know how else he could spend his time and energy anymore. On the occasional days they did not meet, he felt lost and lacked purpose and motivation. Miraj, on the other hand, continued to get bigger and stronger. The more Tim fed him, the bigger he got. The more time they spent together, the more demanding Miraj became. It was an endless cycle. At times, Miraj intimidated Tim into choosing where to go and what game to play. Tim did not eat lunch anymore as there was not enough food for the two of them. He had to sell the wood he gathered for the winter to buy more food for his hungry friend. He had not kept his place clean and tidy, let alone the regular maintenance needed to keep the house in good shape. The ceiling started leaking water when it rained. His flowers died. His chickens became sickly, and his laundry and dishes piled up. He became thin and weak from not eating well and poor from not working enough.

Tim was not totally oblivious to all of that. There were moments of clarity when he looked around and in the mirror and asked himself how he got there! He did not envision this result when he first pursued his friendship with Miraj. He missed his family and friends at times. He missed talking to Wysmin and relaxing in a clean house. He missed having more money. But he knew that every morning, Miraj was expecting them to meet. For a while, he thought that he had control over the relationship. He thought he could leave Miraj anytime there were problems. He thought he could have a good time with Miraj while keeping his life in order at the same time. The fantasy of maintaining a balance between Miraj and his life was so tempting. But such balance was impossible to maintain no matter how hard he tried! The more he tried to reach that balance, the longer he stayed trapped and the more energy and time he lost from his life. And the stronger Miraj became! He eventually realized that the longer he stayed in this relationship, the less control he had over it. It was a trap consuming all of his resources. A big trick! A bottomless pit! The more he tried to fill it, the deeper it became.

*A controlled balance between a healthy lifestyle and addictive behavior
can never be sustained for a long period of time.
The illusion that it can be is merely part of the addiction mentality.
It is another trick the addiction uses
to delay the full recovery.*

As Tim was trying to resolve the situation he found himself in, he wondered if he should accept the problem instead of resisting it. Miraj was a problem only as long as Tim saw him that way. If Tim fully accepted Miraj and identified with him, then fulfilling Miraj's needs would not feel so burdensome. Tim was not sure he wanted Miraj to totally disappear from his life. At the same time, he was not able to have his old life back. Trying to have both Miraj and his old self was difficult and frustrating. Accepting this lifestyle with Miraj and giving up on his old way of living seemed like a logical thing to do. At least this would resolve the uncomfortable conflict within himself. Maybe if Tim embraced his changes instead of resisting them, he would find peace. For days he tried this idea and indeed felt more comfortable meeting with Miraj and fulfilling his demands. He felt less upset by the piled dishes in his kitchen and the scattered dirty laundry in his home. He tried first to ignore it. When he couldn't ignore it, he tried to convince himself that this was the new version of himself, that it did not matter if others liked him this way. Not enough money to buy food? Who cares! He would learn how to scavenge and seize any opportunity to get what he needed. Not getting enough sleep? That is not a problem! He would teach himself to survive on less sleep and even on less food if needed.

He continued to adopt that new identity until one night, he had a scary dream that made him change his mind. He dreamed he woke up with heavy feet. He looked at his hands and they were covered with purple fur. His nails turned into sharp claws. For a moment he felt confused then he felt scared. He ran to the mirror to look at himself and found that his image in the mirror looked like himself. He was terrified but his image in the mirror was smiling at him. He was turning into Miraj on the inside but when he was awake he could not see it. He woke up scared and quickly looked at his hands and felt his face to make sure it was only a dream. The message was clear. The relationship with this creature was changing Tim's identity. The dream represented the truth that he could see. Embracing this relationship meant that he was losing himself. That night he decided that he did not want to lose himself to that monster just because it was easier to surrender and go with the flow. There must be a better way!

Accepting the addiction lifestyle instead of resisting it may ease the psychological conflict. However, it gives the addiction more power and control over one's life.

First attempt to break free

Tim continued to meet with Miraj despite feeling confused, numb, and even distant at times. One morning he woke up exhausted, emotionally and physically. He decided to stay home and let Miraj find his own food that day. That idea gave him a sense of control and freedom. He thought he could easily occupy his day with things to do as there were a lot of things in his life he had neglected. To his surprise, it took some time and effort to think of actual things to do. The usual and easy daily tasks no longer came to mind as second nature, but Miraj popped up in his head all the time! He grabbed a pencil and a piece of paper, tried to focus, and wrote down a list of things to do. They were mostly home chores that were long overdue. He started by making his bed and then did the laundry. After that, he planned to wash the big pile of dirty dishes in the sink. He noticed that it was taking more concentration and energy to do these tasks even though he had done them many times before he met Miraj. It seemed that he had to learn to do them all over again. He struggled but he was making progress. Fresh memories of Miraj were popping up frequently throughout the day and intruding on his plan and interrupting his focus. After managing to complete some of the tasks on his list, he felt some relief and confidence. *Maybe this relationship was not as big of a problem as he thought*, he wondered.

After several hours, he heard a gentle knocking at his door. He opened the door to Miraj looking like the small cute creature from their first meeting. Miraj looked at Tim with a big, warm smile. He grabbed Tim's hand and pulled him gently outside the house inviting Tim to go with him. It seemed as if Miraj had access to Tim's deep needs and wants. Tim had a strong urge to succumb to Miraj and found it hard to resist at first. But Tim promised himself to spend that day at home so he told Miraj no. Miraj did not like to be told no. Tim went inside quickly and closed the door behind him. As he went to resume his chores, Miraj started yelling and banging on the door. Miraj was big again. He was hungry and angry! Tim had been feeding him for months, so was not going to accept "no" for an answer! The door was shaking under his fists as he banged angrily, roaring and demanding food. How could he change from an innocent-looking friend to a huge and furious monster? How did he gain this power to manipulate Tim's mind? Tim tried to ignore him, but the sound was too loud. The little freedom and control he felt that day started to fade away. He tried again to carry on with his home chores and ignore the noise, but he could not focus on his tasks. The banging on his door continued until he could not take it anymore. He grabbed some food, opened the door, and threw it to Miraj who took it all and walked away. The struggle finally stopped. Even though he resisted the temptation to go with Miraj and refused to succumb to all of his demands, he felt exhausted and defeated. The only thing he could do at that point was to go to bed and get more sleep.

Over the next weeks and months, variations of that scenario happened repeatedly and ended with Tim surrendering after initial resistance. Some days, Tim went out with Miraj, and some days he tried to tend to his house. He was not able to do more than basic chores and often he could not complete everything he needed to. Overall, his house was not as clean as before and he was still distant from his family and friends. He had no time to learn new skills or make more money let alone have any hobbies or enjoy new experiences. He could barely do enough to stay alive. He no longer had time and energy to work on future goals to reach his potential in life. He got tired of switching between accepting Miraj in his life and fighting him.

Happy feelings occurred rarely. Happiness at a very basic level requires life's basic needs to be fulfilled, and he no longer had the time and energy to take good care of these needs. Happiness requires a sense of freedom and he was no longer free. Happiness requires a sense of control and he was no longer in control of his life. Happiness often involves seeking higher meaning and purpose such as helping others or growing in knowledge. A life centered on satisfying a greedy creature is devoid of a higher meaning. Tim was unhappy even on a good day. But on bad days, he felt miserable. He was more depressed and anxious than ever. He realized that the creature he initially thought could be a solution to his problems not only failed in helping him but added bigger problems that took on a life of their own. The loud yelling and banging at his door became stronger every time he tried to break free. Most days, he fell into the habit of obeying Miraj's demands automatically without even thinking about it. He was numb. It was easier to surrender to the pressure than to resist. He was giving up.

One night, Tim had a strange but beautiful dream. He dreamt he was diving underwater in a beautiful and clear ocean but he was able to breathe comfortably. His old fish friend, Wysmin suddenly showed up and started talking to him. He was much bigger, almost as big as Tim himself! Or maybe Tim was as small as a fish.

«You are alive!" exclaimed Tim.

Wysmin responded, «I am dead physically, but I am alive in your thoughts.»

«I am sorry I neglected you! I am sorry I lost you!»

«What matters now is to reclaim your life and not lose anymore.»

«I tried, but I fail every time!»

«Every failure is teaching you a new lesson that you can use in your next fight. Every failure is giving you another reason to be stronger so you can succeed the next time."

«How can I succeed and get my life back?»

«You can only succeed if you completely and absolutely end the relationship with this monster and give up on the idea of trying to control it. Instead of controlling the relationship, you have to replace it altogether with better activities and better relationships, even if they don't feel as joyful at first.»

«But how can I do that when his pressure and demands are always distracting me?»

«You need to starve the monster and deprive him of the food and attention that make him stronger. That will weaken him. Then you need to build a fence around you that keeps him away so he cannot tempt you again. At the same time, open the door for your loved ones to connect with you. Fill the void by exploring healthy activities. Start noticing and enjoying the little things in life that you often take for granted. Find meaningful goals and start your journey towards them.»

Tim woke up feeling different that morning. He was more determined and more hopeful. He had two options: one that was easy but costly and one that was difficult but more rewarding. He could continue to live this way and lose himself in the process or choose to reclaim freedom and control over his life.

The first option was easier because he got used to living that way, but it was not what he ultimately wanted for himself. The second option was hard and would take a lot of work, but it was the only way to lasting happiness and meaning in his life. Reclaiming his freedom and control is certainly worth the effort. He realized that if he continued on the same path, he would lose everything. He had lost enough already to the monster he thought was a friend. The only solution was to eradicate the problem and cut the vicious cycle forever. Tim began to realize it takes more than turning the temptation down once in a while.

Recovery is a continuous and active process. It is hard at first but gets easier with time. The wisdom and strength from the journey will enrich one's life and add more meaning and value to it.

Tim took a pen and piece of paper and wrote his plan of recovery:

1.   Starve the monster

2.   Build a fence to keep him away

3.   Fill the void with healthy activities

Starve the monster of addiction to weaken it by not responding to any
of its demands. This eventually will give you back the energy stolen by
addiction and the opportunity to redirect it
to work for you instead of against you.

To be able to control addictive behaviors and thoughts, one has to
carefully identify them first. They are not always clear as they often
masquerade as normal needs.

Identify and heal any past wounds and unmet psychological needs to
decrease the vulnerability to future addictions.

Direct the saved energy, time, and attention to new,
fulfilling goals and activities that keep you occupied leaving none
of it for addiction.

Tim decided that Miraj was not part of who he wanted to be. Miraj was a dysfunctional part of Tim's life that needed to be treated or else it would gradually take over all of his life and end it. He had to label everything he liked or once liked about Miraj in the "unwanted dysfunctional" category and pay attention to his thoughts, feelings, and behaviors so they didn't feed into the cycle he is trying to break. He decided that in order to control something hiding inside, he had to monitor it and understand it first.

The first day Tim did not answer the door to Miraj was very rough. The second and third days were even rougher. The banging was very strong. At times Miraj pleaded and begged. He told Tim that he would never see happiness again unless he agreed to see him and feed him. He tried to entice Tim by reminding him of all the good times they had together and by promising Tim that if they met again, it would be the last time. That particular temptation of "just one more time" was very strong, but Tim was stronger. After a few days, Miraj pretended to give up and to accept Tim's plan to reclaim his life in hopes that Tim would lower his guards but Tim was smarter this time as he knew this trick. Tim continued to follow his plan.

Tim realized that there must be a higher meaning to his existence than being consumed by addiction. He did not exist to spend his life serving Miraj. Even if the meaning of life was still unclear to him, he knew it was not to be the victim of addiction. After a few more days, the pressure to succumb to Miraj began to decrease and continued to decrease gradually over time. Miraj's demands weren't as strong. His voice became less intrusive. His visits became less frequent. Because he was not fed, he became weaker and smaller. Tim watched Miraj through the window sitting and waiting, hoping to find an entrance into Tim's mind again. Tim built a large, strong fence around his house to have a safe space without the temptation of Miraj. His control and power over Tim slowly decreased as Miraj no longer tried to visit every day and with time stopped coming completely. Occasionally, Tim saw and heard him from a distance. This reminded him of the journey they shared with its temporary joys and lasting pains.

When addiction attempts to entice again, it is called cravings. Cravings can lead to relapses if one is vulnerable and not prepared.

As time went by, Tim felt less depressed and more hopeful as he made himself do things outside his addiction. He knew he still had a lot of work to do. He had to work on forgiving himself for losing a portion of his life to that fake relationship. He apologized to his family and friends for neglecting them. He had to recognize the boredom, loneliness, and anxiety that made him vulnerable in the first place and work on them. He realized that he was craving true connection, that he tried to fill the void with the wrong thing. He had to examine how anxiety prevented him from making deeper connections with others. He had to understand how to overcome the barriers that kept him from enjoying the life he had before Miraj and use that to enjoy life now. He looked in the past and present for any wounds that could make him weak again and susceptible to the false promises and temptations of addiction. Working on each one of these things will make him stronger when he comes across Miraj or another cute, little monster in the future! Such encounters and temptations are inevitable in life.

Recovering from a life-hijacking event like addiction
has to be an ongoing and life-long process.

Making new goals and passions

Gradually, Tim had more energy and time to do all the things he wanted to do like taking care of his house and visiting his family and friends. He even got a new fish and enjoyed talking to him every day. He started to discover new joys in the simple things in life, things that have always been there but he did not pay attention to before. For example, feeling the nice morning breeze on his face, hearing the birds sing, and talking and laughing with his family and friends. He became more open to making genuine connections with others. He was more aware of his vulnerabilities and more humbled by them but willing nevertheless to challenge himself to improve and push his limits to be better. He realized that his potential is at the other end of his fears. He started collecting and selling more wood, farming, and making more money. He became more productive and freer! He found joy in giving and helping others. He made a plan that every day he will learn one new thing and do one good thing for himself and others. He reminded himself every morning not to take that day for granted and to be grateful that he was alive and well. He started a daily practice of reflection, gratitude, self-care, and connection with himself and the higher power that helped him recover from his addiction. He realized that in order to progress in life and face its new challenges, he had to grow psychologically and be a little stronger every day.

During the rest of Tim's life, he came across other cute little creatures like Miraj. At times, their innocent appearance almost tricked him but he was more self-aware and focused that he did not succumb to the temptations. Staying busy with important goals in life helped. Focusing and renewing his goals and passions regularly helped. Having a purpose and a higher meaning in his life helped. Staying in touch and truly connecting with his loved ones helped.

He was not immune to life's tricks and temptations. He just had to grow stronger to deal with them. If he happened to fall into the trap of addiction again, he would not let hopelessness seep into his brain and would use the knowledge he accumulated and the skills he learned to escape the traps and learn from them. He realized that staying in control of his life was a precious gift that could not be taken for granted. He was humbled by knowing how easy it was to lose control. But that humility empowered him to value that control and to use it for what mattered most in his life.

Addiction does not happen by choice but choices determine reaching recovery or staying addicted.